The Mezzotint

*A Supernatural Tale of a Haunted
Image
and a Chilling Mystery*

A Modern Translation

Adapted for the Contemporary Reader

M.R. James

Translated by Tim Zengerink

Table of Contents

Preface - Message to the Reader

What If You Could Help Rebuild the Greatest Library in Human History?

Thousands of years ago, the Library of Alexandria stood as the crown jewel of human achievement — a sanctuary where the collected wisdom of every known civilization was gathered, preserved, and shared freely.

And then, it was lost.

Through fire, conquest, and the slow erosion of time, humanity lost not just books — but ideas, dreams, discoveries, and stories that could have changed the world forever.

Today, the Library of Alexandria lives again — and you are invited to be a part of its restoration.

Our mission is simple yet profound:

To rebuild the greatest library the world has ever known, and to translate all timeless works into every language and dialect, so that no seeker of knowledge is ever left behind again.

By joining our movement to rebuild the modern Library of Alexandria, you become part of an unprecedented mission:

- **Unlimited Access to the Greatest Audiobooks & eBooks Ever Written:**

  Instantly explore thousands of legendary works—Plato, Shakespeare, Jane Austen, Leo Tolstoy, and countless more. All instantly available to read or listen, placing a complete literary universe at your fingertips.

- **Beautiful Paperback & Deluxe Editions at Printing Cost**

  Own any title as an elegant paperback, deluxe hardcover, or stunning collectible boxset—offered to you at true printing cost, delivered straight to your door. Build your personal Library of Alexandria, crafted for beauty, built for durability, and worthy of proud display.

- **Fresh Translations for Modern Readers—in Every Language & Dialect**

  Enjoy timeless masterpieces reimagined in clear, contemporary language—no more outdated phrases or obscure references. Alongside the original versions, we're tirelessly translating these classics into every language and dialect imaginable, ensuring accessibility and understanding across cultures and generations.

- **Join a Global Renaissance of Literature & Knowledge**

  You directly support expanding our library, publishing deluxe editions at true cost, translating works into all global languages, and bringing humanity's greatest stories to people everywhere. By joining today, you're not just preserving a legacy of masterpieces; you set in motion a powerful wave of literary accessibility.

Become a Torchbearer of Knowledge.

Join us for free now at **LibraryofAlexandria.com**

Together, we will ensure that the light of human wisdom never fades again.

With gratitude and a shared love of knowledge,

The Modern Library of Alexandria Team

Visit:

www.libraryofalexandria.com

Or scan the code below:

Introduction

The Haunted Image and
the Terror of Silent Retribution

M.R. James's The Mezzotint, first published in his debut collection Ghost Stories of an Antiquary (1904), is one of the finest examples of his mastery over understated supernatural horror. A quiet yet deeply unsettling tale, it is centered on an engraving—a seemingly ordinary, static image—that slowly and inexplicably changes over time, revealing a disturbing story embedded within its shifting lines. This eerie premise allows James to explore one of his favorite narrative mechanisms: the gradual unfolding of supernatural terror through arcane objects, scholarly curiosity, and the slow encroachment of dread into the orderly world of the academic.

Unlike many ghost stories that rely on dramatic apparitions or visceral horror, The Mezzotint is remarkable for its restraint and ingenuity. There is no blood, no violent confrontation, and no immediate threat. Instead, James conjures fear through atmosphere, suggestion, and the uncanny—the sense that the natural order of things has been subtly, but irreversibly, broken. A mezzotint is a type of engraved image known for its rich tonal gradation, especially in depicting shadows. James cleverly uses this medium as both metaphor and mechanism for his ghost: something dark taking shape not in sudden motion, but in creeping progression.

The story takes place within the refined halls of academia, a world of librarians, museum curators, and antiquarians. When an art curator acquires a curious mezzotint of an English manor, the image appears to contain more than just artistic rendering—it seems to depict an unfolding narrative. Figures begin to appear in the image who were not previously there, and the scene subtly changes over hours and days, telling the story of a supernatural vengeance being carried out before the very eyes of the unsuspecting characters. But no one can stop it. They can only watch.

This introduction will explore the enduring brilliance of The Mezzotint—its themes, structure, and impact—while placing it within the wider context of M.R. James's work and the ghost story tradition. We will examine James's use of suggestion over spectacle, the symbolism of the haunted image, and the emotional undercurrents of justice, loss, and historical trauma that animate the tale. We'll also explore the story's unique legacy in shaping modern horror, especially in its anticipations of visual media as a medium for supernatural storytelling. The Mezzotint is not just about what is seen—it's about the terror of seeing something that shouldn't be moving, something that shouldn't exist. And that horror—quiet, creeping, unanswerable—is James at his most masterful.

A Ghost in the Frame:
Storytelling through Art and Atmosphere

The central conceit of The Mezzotint is deceptively simple: an academic discovers that a newly acquired engraving appears to change over time, depicting a ghostly revenge. But within that simplicity lies a tightly crafted mechanism of suspense and philosophical reflection. The protagonist, Mr. Williams, is a curator at a university museum—an educated, rational man who finds himself unnerved not by a dramatic haunting, but by an image that refuses to stay still.

James builds tension not through shock, but through a steady escalation of the uncanny. When the mezzotint first arrives, it is noted as dull, depicting an ordinary country house with no particular artistic value. But upon subsequent viewings, strange details begin to emerge—a dark figure at the edge of the scene, a small bundle, an open window. The horror grows as the image slowly reveals a grim story: a cloaked man approaching the house, abducting a child from within, and vanishing into the distance. Each observer sees a new stage of the sequence, which cannot be reversed or hurried, as if the image is telling its own story at its own pace.

This use of a static medium as a dynamic narrative device is one of James's most innovative contributions to supernatural fiction. By choosing a mezzotint—an obsolete, shadow-heavy form of engraving—he evokes a sense of antiquarian obscurity, something halfway between art and relic. The supernatural is thus not outside the frame of civilization, but embedded in its very symbols. It's not just that something is wrong with the image—it's that the image itself is a record of a wrong. A curse, printed in silence.

The horror here is voyeuristic and helpless. The characters are observers, not participants. They cannot intervene in the image's unfolding tragedy; they can only bear witness. And this is a key theme in James's work: the idea that certain knowledge carries no power, only burden. The image becomes a ghost in itself—a haunted object that plays out its tale of revenge again and again, for those curious or unlucky enough to see it.

James's language throughout is precise and matter-of-fact, grounded in scholarly dialogue and genteel observation. This tonal restraint contrasts sharply with the content of the image, and it is in that contrast—between decorum and dread—that the story gains much of its power. The haunting is not dramatic. It is quiet, meticulous, and inevitable. And like a mezzotint, the more you stare at it, the darker it becomes.

The Legacy of Violence: Justice, Vengeance, and the Persistence of the Past

Beneath the eerie mechanism of the mezzotint lies a moral and historical engine that drives the horror: the idea that certain acts—especially acts of injustice—do not simply vanish. They remain. They imprint themselves on the world. And sometimes, they find a way to speak again.

As the story unfolds, the characters uncover the historical backstory of the haunted image. The house depicted in the mezzotint once belonged to a family named Gawdy. Generations earlier, the family executed a poacher for alleged trespass and theft. The poacher's son, embittered and desperate, was later caught attempting to steal a child from the Gawdy estate—presumably in retribution or madness—and was executed for the crime. But it is this son who returns in the mezzotint, cloaked in darkness, reenacting the very act that cost him his life.

The supernatural element, then, is not random—it is retributive. It is a return of the repressed, the past made visible through an unexplainable medium. The ghost is not merely a figure of fear, but of historical consequence. The crime—whether murder or injustice—was buried in time, but it was never truly resolved. The mezzotint becomes a visual echo of that trauma, a grim justice etched in ink and shadow.

This idea—that certain truths remain restless—is central to James's vision of horror. His ghosts are rarely vague spooks; they are emissaries of judgment. But they do not speak in moral terms. They appear, they act, they punish. In The Mezzotint, the story is over before the characters understand it. They are latecomers to a drama that has already ended. Their role is not to stop it, but to learn—too late—what it meant.

And this is part of the deeper fear in James's work: that knowledge, especially of the occult or the forgotten, comes without power. It is not liberating—it is damning. To discover the truth is not to solve a mystery, but to expose oneself to forces that do not care if one understands. The story ends not with exorcism or revelation, but with resignation. The mezzotint is returned to its sender, the mystery left intact, the horror still contained—waiting, perhaps, for the next viewer.

In this way, The Mezzotint reflects a broader theme in James's fiction: the fragility of modern certainty in the face of ancient wrongs. The past is not dead. It waits in books, in stones, in images. And when disturbed, it speaks again.

A Mirror to Modern Horror: Influence and Enduring Appeal

The Mezzotint is a masterpiece not just because of what it does, but because of how it continues to resonate. Its influence stretches far beyond its time, anticipating themes that would dominate 20th- and 21st-century horror: cursed media, found footage, haunted photographs, and the idea that visual technology can become a vessel for the supernatural. Stories like The Ring, Sinister, and Antrum all bear traces of James's story—tales where the act of viewing becomes an invitation to dread.

But James's contribution is deeper than plot. His narrative philosophy—of suggestion over spectacle, of dread over shock—remains foundational to literary horror. He never over-explains, never names the supernatural fully. He respects the unknown. And in doing so, he leaves a space for the reader's imagination to do the final, most terrifying work.

In The Mezzotint, James also reflects on the very nature of storytelling. The mezzotint is a narrative—it has a beginning, middle, and end. But it is mute. It doesn't explain itself. The characters must piece it together, infer its meaning, and interpret its silence. This mirrors the ghost story itself: a tale told not to resolve fear, but to awaken it.

For the modern reader, the story remains a chilling experience not because of what is shown, but because of what is implied. It reminds us that not all knowledge is safe, not all stories are ours to tell, and not all images are still. In a world increasingly saturated with moving pictures, James's tale feels eerily prescient.

The Mezzotint is not merely about a haunted artwork—it is about the art of haunting. It is about the things that move in silence, that unfold unseen, and that leave us staring, helpless, at something we cannot explain.

And when we finally look away, we are not sure if the image is done with us—or if it is still changing, just out of sight.

The Mezzotint

A while back, I shared a strange story about my friend Dennistoun and something that happened to him while he was collecting art for the Cambridge museum. He didn't share many details after returning to England, but over time, the story spread among his friends— especially to one man who ran an art museum at a different university.

This man, who I'll call Mr. Williams, had a job similar to Dennistoun's, and the story left a strong impression on him. He was glad, though, that his job didn't require him to collect old manuscripts like Dennistoun did. That was the job of the Shelburnian Library. They could go searching dusty corners of Europe for that kind of thing if they wanted. Mr. Williams, meanwhile, was happy to stick with English topographical drawings and engravings—pictures of buildings and landscapes—something he thought was much safer. But even that quiet line of work had its own dark corners, and Mr. Williams was about to stumble into one of them.

Anyone who's interested in collecting old prints of places in England knows about one London dealer in particular—Mr. J. W. Britnell. He regularly puts out catalogs full of drawings, maps, and engravings of churches, houses, and towns from all over England and Wales. Mr. Williams used these catalogs all the time. Since his museum already had a huge collection, he didn't buy often, but he did rely on Mr. Britnell to fill in any gaps.

In February of last year, Mr. Williams received a new catalog from Mr. Britnell, along with a short typed note that said:

Dear Sir,

Please take a look at item No. 978 in the catalog we've sent. We'd be happy to send it to you for review if you're interested.

Yours faithfully,

J. W. Britnell

Mr. Williams quickly flipped to entry No. 978. It read:

978.—Unknown. Interesting mezzotint: View of a manor-house, early part of the century. 15 by 10 inches; black frame. £2 2s.

It didn't sound especially interesting, and the price seemed a little high. But Mr. Britnell usually knew what he was doing, and if he thought it was worth recommending, it might be worth a look. So Mr. Williams sent back a postcard asking to see the mezzotint, along with a few other items listed in the catalog. Then he got back to his usual work, not thinking much more about it.

As often happens, the package didn't arrive until later than expected—Saturday afternoon, after Mr. Williams had already left work. The museum's attendant brought it to his college rooms so he wouldn't have to wait until Monday. It was waiting there when he came back for tea with a friend.

The only item that really matters here is the mezzotint in the black frame. That's the one mentioned in the catalog. I'll do my best to describe it, though I can't make you see it as clearly as I can still picture it myself.

The print looked a lot like those you can still find hanging in old village inns or in the hallways of country houses that haven't changed in decades. It wasn't a very good mezzotint—and a bad mezzotint is probably the worst kind of print you can find. It showed a manor house, viewed from the front. The house wasn't very large, and it looked like it was from the 1700s. It had three rows of plain windows, with decorative stonework around them, and a small porch in the center. There were trees on both sides of the house and a large lawn in front. At the bottom, it said "A. W. F. sculpsit," meaning someone with those initials had made the engraving. There was no title or description.

It looked like the work of an amateur artist. Mr. Williams couldn't understand why Mr. Britnell thought it was worth over two pounds. He turned the picture over with a bit of scorn. On the back was a paper label, but part of it had been torn off. All that was left were the ends of two lines:

The first said: —ngley Hall

The second: —ssex

It wasn't much to go on.

He figured it might be worth trying to figure out what place was shown in the picture. With a gazetteer, that would be easy. Then he could return the picture to Mr. Britnell and make a few comments about the dealer's poor taste.

It was already dark, so he lit some candles, made tea, and served it to a friend he'd played golf with earlier. (Apparently, the university staff enjoy golf for fun.) While they had tea, they talked about their game—a conversation that any golfer could imagine, but which I'll spare non-golfers from reading.

They agreed that they both could've made better shots and didn't get the luck they deserved in some situations. Around that time, the friend—let's call him Professor Binks—picked up the framed picture and asked:

"What's this place, Williams?"

"That's exactly what I'm trying to figure out," Williams replied, grabbing a gazetteer off the shelf. "Check the back. It says something-Hall, maybe in Sussex or Essex. But the first part of the name is torn off. You don't recognize it, do you?"

"It's from that guy Britnell, right?" said Binks. "Is it for the museum?"

"Well, I might buy it if it cost five shillings," said Williams. "But for some odd reason, he wants two guineas. I don't get it. It's a bad engraving, and there aren't even any people in it to make it interesting."

"I wouldn't say it's worth two guineas," Binks replied, "but I don't think it's terrible. The moonlight looks pretty well done. And I thought I saw a figure— right at the edge in the front."

"Let's take a look," said Williams. "Well, you're right—the lighting is actually pretty good. Where do you see the figure? Oh yeah! Just a head, right at the bottom of the picture."

Sure enough, there was something—just a small dark shape at the edge of the image. It looked like the head of a man or woman, wrapped in something, with their back turned, staring at the house.

Williams hadn't noticed that before.

"Still," he said, "even though it's better than I thought, I can't spend museum money on a picture of a house I can't even name."

Professor Binks had other work to do, so he soon left. Williams kept trying to figure out the name of the place in the picture, but he had no luck. "If only I could see the letter before the 'ng,' it'd be easy," he thought. "But now the name could be anything—Guestingley, Langley—there are way more possibilities than I expected. And this awful book doesn't even have an index for place name endings."

Dinner (called Hall at the college) was at seven. It doesn't need much description, especially since the people there were also golfers and kept talking about the game.

After dinner, Williams spent some time in the common room, and later, a few guests came back to his room. They likely played whist and smoked. At one point, during a break in the evening, Williams picked up the mezzotint without thinking and handed it to someone mildly interested in art. He told him where it came from and repeated the details we already know.

The guest glanced at it, then said with growing interest, "This is actually a really good piece, Williams. It feels like something from the romantic era. The lighting is excellent, and even though the figure's a bit creepy, it's strangely powerful."

"Yes, isn't it?" Williams said from across the room as he poured drinks for the others and didn't come over to look at it again.

It was getting late, and soon everyone left. Williams had to write a couple of letters and finish some leftover tasks. Finally, a bit after midnight, he was ready for bed. He turned off his lamp after lighting his bedroom candle. The picture was still face-up on the table where the last guest had left it, and he happened to glance at it just as he turned down the lamp.

What he saw made him nearly drop the candle in shock. He says that if the room had gone completely dark just then, he might've passed out from fear. But since he still had light, he carefully set the candle down and looked closer.

There was no mistake—although it seemed completely impossible, it was true.

There was now a figure in the middle of the lawn in front of the house. It hadn't been there earlier at five o'clock. The figure was crawling on its hands and knees toward the house. It wore a weird black outfit with a white cross on the back.

He wasn't sure what the best thing to do was, but here's what Mr. Williams decided. He picked up the picture by one corner, carried it across the hallway to his second set of rooms, and locked it in a drawer. Then he locked both sets of doors and got ready for bed. But before sleeping, he wrote and signed a note explaining the strange change he had seen in the picture since he received it.

It took him a while to fall asleep, but at least he felt better knowing someone else had also noticed something odd in the picture the night before. If not, he might've thought he was losing his mind. Since that wasn't the case, he had two things to do the next day: carefully study the picture again with a witness, and try to figure out what house was shown in it. He decided to invite his neighbor, Nisbet, for breakfast and then spend the morning looking through a gazetteer.

Nisbet was free and showed up around 9:30. Williams wasn't quite dressed yet, which was a little embarrassing. At breakfast, Williams didn't mention the picture, except to say he wanted Nisbet's opinion on one. If you know anything about university life, you can guess the conversation went off in all sorts of directions—golf, tennis, and more. Still, Williams seemed distracted. He was clearly thinking about the strange image locked in the drawer across the hall.

Finally, after breakfast and a morning smoke, it was time. Excited and a little nervous, Williams rushed across the hall, opened the drawer, grabbed the picture (still face down), and brought it back for Nisbet to look at.

"Now," Williams said, "tell me exactly what you see in that picture. Be as detailed as you can. I'll explain why later."

"Well," said Nisbet, "I see a view of a country house—looks English—at night under the moon."

"Moonlight? You're sure?"

"Yes. The moon looks like it's getting smaller. And there are clouds."

"Okay, go on." Williams muttered to himself, "There wasn't any moon when I looked at it the first time."

"Well, not much more to say," Nisbet went on. "The house has three rows of windows, five in each, except the bottom row where there's a porch instead of a center window."

"What about any people?" Williams asked quickly.

"There aren't any."

"What? No figure on the lawn?"

"Nothing at all."

"You're sure?"

"Of course. But... wait—one of the windows on the ground floor, left side, is open."

"Is it really? Then he must have gotten inside!" Williams exclaimed. He hurried over, took the picture from Nisbet, and checked for himself.

It was true. The lawn was empty, but one window was now open. Williams stood in shock for a moment, then rushed to his desk and wrote for a bit. He brought two papers back to Nisbet—one was the description Nisbet had just given, and the other was the note

Williams had written the night before. He asked Nisbet to sign the first one, then read the second.

"What does it all mean?" Nisbet asked.

"That's exactly the question," said Williams. "I need to do three things. First, find out from Garwood"—the friend who had seen the picture the night before—"what he saw. Second, get a photo of this thing before it changes again. And third, find out where this house is."

"I can take the photo," said Nisbet. "But you know, it feels like we're witnessing some kind of crime play out. The question is—did it already happen, or is it going to?"

Williams looked at the picture again. "You're right. He's inside now. And I've got a bad feeling about what's going to happen upstairs."

"I'll take this to old Green," Williams said. Green was the senior fellow who had been in charge of college property for years. "He might recognize the place—we own land in Essex and Sussex, and he's traveled a lot through both."

"He might," said Nisbet, "but I think he's out of town. He wasn't at dinner last night, and I heard he went to Brighton for the weekend."

"You're right," said Williams. "Well, take the photo now, and I'll go talk to Garwood and get his side of things. Keep an eye on the picture while I'm gone. At this point, two guineas feels like a bargain."

He soon returned, bringing Garwood with him. Garwood said he had seen the figure just stepping off the edge of the picture and heading onto the lawn. He remembered a white mark on the back of the figure's clothing, though he couldn't tell if it was a cross. They wrote up his statement and had him sign it, and then Nisbet took the photo of the picture.

"What are you going to do now?" Nisbet asked. "Are you going to sit and watch it all day?"

"Well, no, I don't think so," said Williams. "I have a feeling we're supposed to watch this whole thing unfold. Between last night and this morning, enough time passed for a lot to happen, but the thing in the picture only made it into the house. If it had finished whatever it came to do, it probably would've left by now. But since the window is still open, I think it's still inside. So I'm not too worried about leaving it alone. Besides, I don't think it'll change much, if at all, during the day. We can go for a walk this afternoon and check on it again when we come back for tea—or when it starts getting dark. I'll leave it out here on the table and lock the door. My servant can get in, but no one else."

They all agreed that this plan made sense. They also thought it would be better to stick together for the rest of the day, so they wouldn't be tempted to tell anyone else about the strange picture. If rumors got out, it could attract the attention of the Phasmatological Society, which they didn't want.

Let's leave them there until around five o'clock.

Around that time, the three of them returned to Williams's rooms. At first, they were annoyed to see the door wasn't locked, but then remembered that the servants usually came earlier on Sundays to check in. But something unexpected was waiting for them.

The picture was still there on the table, leaning against a stack of books, just as they had left it. But across from it sat Williams's servant—Mr. Filcher— staring at the picture with a look of pure horror on his face.

This was strange. Mr. Filcher was a well-respected servant, known for his perfect manners. Sitting in his master's chair and showing interest in his master's belongings was completely unlike him. He seemed to realize this too, because he jumped up quickly when they entered and said:

"Sorry, sir, I shouldn't have sat down like that."

"That's all right, Robert," said Williams. "Actually, I wanted to ask what you thought of that picture."

"Well, sir, I wouldn't put it somewhere my little girl could see it. Not if you ask me."

"Really? Why not?"

"Well, sir, I remember once she saw a picture in an old Bible that wasn't even half as bad as this, and we had to stay up with her three or four nights after that. If she saw something like this—some skeleton or whatever it is carrying off a baby—she'd be scared out of her mind. Kids get frightened over the smallest things. But I just don't think this is the kind of picture that should be lying around where someone might stumble on it. Will you need anything else tonight, sir? Thank you, sir."

With that, Mr. Filcher left, and the three men rushed to look at the picture. There was the house, lit by the pale moon with clouds drifting by. The window that had been open earlier was now closed. But the figure had returned—it was no longer crawling. Now it stood upright, walking quickly toward the front of the picture.

The moonlight was behind it, and its long black robe hung over its face, hiding most of it. What little they could see was enough: a pale, round forehead and a few wisps of hair. It clutched something tightly in its arms—a child, though it was hard to tell if the child was alive or not. Its legs were thin and bony, and the whole image was deeply disturbing.

From five until seven, they took turns watching the picture. But nothing changed. They finally decided it was safe to leave it again and agreed to come back after dinner to see what happened next.

When they returned as soon as they could, the picture was still there—but the figure was gone. The house stood quietly under the moonlight once more. With nothing else to do, they spent the evening flipping through guidebooks, trying to identify the place. At 11:30 p.m., Williams found what he was looking for in Murray's Guide to Essex:

"16½ miles—Anningley. The church, originally Norman, was remodeled in a classical style in the last century. It holds the tombs of the Francis family. Their home, Anningley Hall, a solid Queen Anne-style house, stands just beyond the churchyard in a park of 80 acres. The family is now extinct. The last heir vanished mysteriously as a baby in 1802. His father, Arthur Francis, was a skilled amateur mezzotint engraver. After the child's disappearance, he lived alone at the Hall and was found dead in his studio exactly three years later, having just finished an engraving of the house. Copies of the print are very rare."

That was enough proof. When Mr. Green returned from his trip, he confirmed the house was indeed Anningley Hall.

Williams asked, "Is there any explanation for the figure?"

Green replied, "I'm not sure. But when I first knew the area, people used to say this: old Francis hated poachers and would get anyone he suspected kicked off his land. One man, though, managed to avoid being caught. He was the last of an old local family—used to be lords of the manor, I think. That made him bitter, especially because he had family tombs in the church. But Francis could never get him—until one day the keepers caught him hunting in a far-off corner of the estate."

Green leaned closer. "There was a fight. The man's name was Gawdy. He ended up shooting one of the keepers. That was all Francis needed. Back then, juries didn't ask many questions. Gawdy was hanged right away. They buried him on the north side of the churchyard—where they put people who were hanged or committed suicide. People used to say that one of

Gawdy's friends must've tried to get revenge by taking Francis's baby. But honestly, I think it was Gawdy himself. Gives me chills to think about it. Have a drink, Williams."

Williams shared everything with his friend Dennistoun, who later told the story to a group that included me—and a certain professor who dismissed it all by saying, "Oh, those Bridgeford folks will believe anything." That remark got exactly the cold reaction it deserved.

The picture is now kept at the Ashleian Museum. Experts tested it to see if invisible ink had been used, but found nothing. Mr. Britnell, the dealer, knew little about it, except that it was rare. Though closely watched ever since, the picture has never changed again.

The End

Thank You for Reading

Dear Reader,

We hope this timeless classic has sparked your imagination and enriched your literary journey. Now that you've turned the final page, we want to share a vision for the future of reading—one where every classic you've ever wanted to explore is at your fingertips, in a format that best suits your life.

We'd like to invite you to gain immediate, unlimited digital & audiobook access to hundreds of the most treasured literary classics ever written—along with the option to secure deluxe paperback, hardcover & box set editions at printing cost. Together, we can spark a new global literary renaissance alongside our small, independent publishing house called "The Library of Alexandria."

Thousands of years ago, the Library of Alexandria stood as a beacon of knowledge—until it was lost to history. We aim to reignite that spirit of preservation and discovery right now, in the modern age—only this time, it's accessible to all, in every language and every format.

Picture a world where every timeless classic, novel, poem, or philosophical treatise is not only available to read but also updated for today's readers—modernized, translated into any language or dialect, and ready to enjoy in any format you choose, whether that is in an eBook, audiobook, paperback, or deluxe hardcover & box set version a printing cost.

By joining our movement to rebuild the modern Library of Alexandria, you become part of an unprecedented mission to offer:

- **Unlimited Audiobook & eBook Access to the Greatest Classics of All Time**

  Instantly explore thousands of legendary works, from Plato and Shakespeare to Jane Austen and Leo Tolstoy. All are instantly ready to read or listen to, giving you a complete literary universe at your fingertips.

- **Paperback & Deluxe Editions at Printing Costs:**

  Purchase any title in a paperback, deluxe hardbound, or deluxe boxset edition at printing costs, shipped right to your doorstep. Curate your personal library of Alexandria with editions worthy of display— crafted to last, designed to captivate, and delivered straight to your door.

- **Modern translations for Contemporary Readers in all languages and dialects**

  Discover a vast selection of classics reimagined in clear, current language—no more struggling with outdated phrases or obscure references. Next to the original versions, we aim to offer translations in as many languages and dialects as possible.

  As we continue our translation efforts and add new languages, readers everywhere can connect with these works as if they were written today. By bridging linguistic divides, you're contributing to ensuring that these timeless stories become more meaningful, accessible, and inspiring for people across the globe.

- **Your Personal Library of Alexandria:**

  Over the months and years, you'll curate a unique physical archive of classics—each volume a testament to your taste, curiosity, and love of knowledge. It's not just about owning books—it's about curating a cultural legacy you'll cherish and pass down for generations to come.

- **Join a Global Literary Renaissance:**

  Your support fuels an ongoing mission: allowing us to reinvest in offering deluxe print editions (including special boxsets) at their true cost, broaden the range of available formats and translations, and extend the reach of these works to new audiences worldwide. By joining today, you're not just preserving a legacy of masterpieces; you set in motion a powerful wave of literary accessibility.

We are more than a publisher—we're a movement, and we can't do it alone. Your support lets us scale our mission, preserving and reimagining history's greatest works for tomorrow's readers.

Become a Torchbearer of knowledge.

Thank you for picking up this book and allowing us into your literary journey. As you turn the pages, know that you're part of something larger: a global effort to keep these stories alive, share their wisdom across borders and generations, and spark a true cultural revival for the modern era.

If this resonates with you—please consider taking the next step by visiting:

www.libraryofalexandria.com

With gratitude and a shared love of knowledge,

The Modern Library of Alexandria Team

Visit:

www.libraryofalexandria.com

Or scan the code below: